For Teri. I love you more than pinkdrinkers love pink.

Sail on, Silvergirl.

I Love You More Than the Smell of Swamp Gas

Copyright © 2017 by Kevan Atteberry. All rights reserved. Manufactured in China. No part of this book may be used or reproduced in any manner whatsoever without written permission except in the case of brief quotations embodied in critical articles and reviews. For information address HarperCollins Children's Books, a division of HarperCollins Publishers, 195 Broadway, New York, NY 10007. www.harpercollinschildrens.com. Library of Congress Control Number: 2016957940 ISBN 978-0-06-240871-6

The artist used Adobe Photoshop to create the digital illustrations for this book. Typography by Erica De Chavez

17 18 19 20 21 SCP 10 9 8 7 6 5 4 3 2 1 ❖ First Edition

I LOVE YOU
More Than the Smell of
SWAMP GAS

Kevan Atteberry

HARPER

An Imprint of HarperCollinsPublishers

I **LOVE** nothing more
than a midnight romp
while I chase wild skink
through the dark, stinky swamp.

Do you love me as much
as the SKINK that you chase
or the SMELL of the swamp
or the BEASTS in this place?

OH! I love you much more
than this swamp or wild skink.

I love you, MY NEWTLING,
much more than you think.

Do you love me as much
as the BUBBLING SLIME
that covers our feet
in a THICK GOOEY GRIME?

I treasure you more
than the SLOW OOZING MUCK
squished through our toes
as we pull them unstuck.

I love you as much . . .

as **bloodsucking ducks.**

Do you love me as much
as the the GAS being sprayed
by this PURPLE-HORNED SKUNK
that I'm shooing away?

I adore you as much
as the SMELL OF SWAMP GAS!
A STENCH so delightful
we don't want to pass.

And I love you, MY STINKLING . . .

like
mummified bass.

Do you love me as much
as the CLICKETY-CLACK
of a skeleton's jig
in a hat TALL and BLACK?

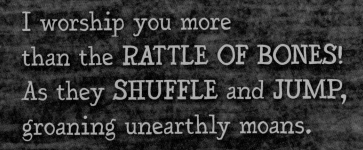

I worship you more
than the RATTLE OF BONES!
As they SHUFFLE and JUMP,
groaning unearthly moans.

I love you, MY DRUMLING . . .

more than **toe-biting stones.**

Do you love me as much
as GHOST BATS in flight
as they whip 'round our heads
in the GLOWING MOONLIGHT?

I cherish you more than
the ghost bats in air
as they dive after GHOST IMPS
infesting our hair.

You're twice as much fun . . . .

as TWO
two-headed
bears.

Do you love me as much
as a **TWISTED DEAD TREE**,
whose gnarled branches reach out
to grab you and me?

I relish you more than
the DARK SERENADE
the BASILISKS belch
to the eggs they have laid.

I love you as much . . .

as a **spider parade**.

Do you love me as much
as the CREATURES AT NIGHT
that follow us,
scurrying out of the light?

I am drawn to you more
than that RASCAL FULL MOON
playing tricks with your eyes
where dark shadows are strewn.

I love you, MY GHOSTLING . . .

more than
moonstruck raccoons.

Do you love me
as much as DESSERT BEFORE BED?
I think that you must
after all that you've said.

Dessert before bed?
Hmmm, let me see. . . .
Well . . .
I DO!

I do love you more
than a bowl full of bees
drizzled with SLIME and
sprinkled with FLEAS.

I love you,
MY CHILDLING . . .